Nazis, Holocaust, and *Self-Love*

PREVIOUSLY PUBLISHED WITH
RESOURCE PUBLICATIONS

Nonfiction

Storms Are Faith's Workout: Preparing Christians for Spiritual Ambush (2018).
Faith's Journey Confronts Obstacles: Instructing God's Soldiers to Overcome in His Armor (2019).
Satan's Strategy to Torment Through Physical Ambush: Educating God's Soldiers of Satan's Plot to Shatter Faith through Sickness and Disease (2019).
Spiritual Shipwreck on the Horizon: Exhorting Christians to Contend for the Faith and Comprehend the Deceitfulness of Sin (2019).
Satan Has No Authority Over God's Soldier: Illuminating Godlike Faith (2019).
God: The Holy Spirit: The Conquering Power Within (2019).
Signs of the Time: Warning: Lukewarm Christianity Accepts Deception (2020)
Flesh and Spirit Conflict: The Inner Battle of Choice (2020).

Fiction

The Elfdins and the Gold Temple: An Oralee Chronicle (2018).
Charlie McGee and the Leprechaun: Life's Curious Twist of Events (2019).
The Shrines of Manitoba: Dark Secrets Shall Be Brought to Light (2019).
Guilty As Blood: One Can Make a Difference (2019).
Back From the Dead: Light Shines As the Noonday Sun (2020).

Nazis, Holocaust, and *Self-Love*

Unbridled Bigotry

R. C. JETTE

RESOURCE *Publications* • Eugene, Oregon

NAZIS, HOLOCAUST, AND SELF-LOVE
Unbridled Bigotry

All Scriptures mentioned are from the KING JAMES VERSION (KJV): KING JAMES VERSION, public domain.

Resource Publications
An Imprint of Wipf and Stock Publishers
199 W. 8th Ave., Suite 3
Eugene, OR 97401

www.wipfandstock.com

PAPERBACK ISBN: 978-1-7252-7854-7
HARDCOVER ISBN: 978-1-7252-7855-4
EBOOK ISBN: 978-1-7252-7856-1

Manufactured in the U.S.A.   05/18/20

This book is dedicated to my Lord Jesus Christ
to whom I am eternally grateful.

I am deeply indebted to Paul, my husband, who has
encouraged and supported me in my writing endeavor.
My daughter, Dawn, who has been an incredible help in
freeing me up to write, and Mike and Susanna
for their continued help and prayers.

I would also like to mention my daughter Christina and my
grandsons, Andrew, Matthew, and Joshua, and my son PJ
and my granddaughter, Kierra. Also, to those who have gone
before me (Mom, Carol, Frank, Raymond, Sarah, etc.) what a
glorious reunion day is ahead.

I give special thanks to Wipf and Stock Publishers for the
phenomenal help in bringing my dream to be an author to
fruition. Heartfelt thanks to Matthew Wimer, George Callihan,
Shannon Carter, and Savanah Landerholm to whom words
cannot express my gratitude.

BROTHERHOOD

Before calm can grace the world,
Unity must be our foundation;
Separation through strife breeds like cancer,
And the core of brotherhood is overthrown.

Mankind's the highest of earth's creation,
Yet discord condescends to the base;
Diversity is part of human complexity,
Commending man's uniqueness.

Male and female constitute society,
The color of skin is outward;
Humanity is not according to race,
For all are made of flesh and blood.

We must rise up in one accord,
And conquer the foe of hate and prejudice;
Permit all to express their opinion,
Not in hostility, but as comrades.

—R. C. JETTE

Contents

Introduction

ALTHOUGH THIS BOOK REVEALS Nazism and the Holocaust that came about in World War II, it's meant as a foundation to illuminate what is happening today. There is a need for blinders to fall off and truth to be seen. We must be aware of the evil that's transpiring in our own country and the world. But first, we must ask ourselves, "How does such evil come about? How did the Holocaust come about?"

> This know also, that in the last days perilous times shall come, For men shall be lovers of their own selves, covetous, boasters, proud, blasphemers, disobedient to parents, unthankful, unholy, Without natural affection, truce-breakers, false accusers, incontinent, fierce, despisers of those that are good, Traitors, heady, highminded, lovers of pleasures more than lovers of God (2 Timothy 3:1–4).

While we must love ourselves to take care of our well-being, it must not be a self-love that is concerned only about our pleasures, wants, or desires to the neglect of others.

Let me explain what the self-love in the scripture above is referring to. That sort of lover of self is the root of the selfishness that brought about the holocaust and the evil that pursued. It's the self-absorbed, egotistical, self-obsessed type of loving self that disregards others.

When the love of self becomes self-centered, desires an excessive need for admiration, disregards the feelings of others, is unable to handle any criticism, and demands privilege, that's when it becomes selfishness. It is no longer a Biblical love of self (Matthew 22:39).

The lover of self that produces perilous times is when we are self-centered, self-obsessed, or preoccupied with self. It's being concerned excessively or exclusively for oneself or one's own advantage, pleasure, or welfare. When we are self-focused, we tend to ignore the needs of others and only do what's best for us. If we become a lover of self or selfish, we suffer from the "ME" syndrome where all that matters is my happiness, my satisfaction, my well-being, what "I" want or desire with little or no concern for the well-being, happiness, etc. of others.

Self-love, selfishness, or self-centeredness is the cause of all the evil brought forth from man. Man murdering due to hate, bigotry, jealousy, anger, etc. is selfishness or self-love. That was revealed in Cain murdering Able (Genesis 4:5–10). Murdering the unborn and newborn in abortion because it would interfere with "my" life is selfishness or self-love. Rape is another form of selfishness or self-love that is concerned with "me" and only me with no care of the trauma to its victims. Stealing, lying, homosexuality, fornication, adultery, gossip, etc. are all the result of selfishness or self-love. Selfishness is an unhealthy love of self that centers on "Me" and satisfying my desires and my pleasures in life with no concern of its consequences, its cost, its effects to others.

Some may be thinking the Scripture text in 2 Timothy is talking about the last days. I believe the perilous times of the last days began with the day of Pentecost and the pouring out of the Holy Spirit that officially began the end times spoken of in Joel chapter two. Yes, Pentecost happened about 2,000 years ago, but Scripture settles that also.

> But, beloved, be not ignorant of this one thing, that one day is with the Lord as a thousand years, and a thousand years as one day (2 Peter 3:8).

We are in the last days according to the Lord. During this time, there will be perilous, dangerous, extreme happenings. The persecution of the early church, the Holocaust of Hitler and the Nazi Party during World War II, all the horrors we hear about daily are described in Scripture as perilous times as men become lovers of self and so self-absorbed that they abuse their fellow humanity.

The intention of this book is to reveal the dangers of being a lover of self or selfish. It must be understood that the self-love in 2 Timothy is an unhealthy concern for only "ME" and disregards the needs of others. It's my objective to enlighten the dangers of socialism, communism, etc. through the use of the Holocaust and Nazi Germany. Through the help of this historical happening, I will unfold a story of the evil and unbridled bigotry that selfishness or self-love unleashes.

What I have done to bring this truth forth is to incorporate historical facts, fictional historical letters written from a son to his mother, and poetry reflecting the struggle and confusion during his false imprisonment in Poland. Then his tribulation, anguish, and turmoil from the conflict of flesh and spirit raging within as his faith is sorely tested in Auschwitz concentration camp.

My intention is to help us comprehend the suffering that took place in the concentration camps. Therefore, I have given some historical verities. In between these truths, I've entwined a story about a young man who knows scriptural truth and is battered daily by a depraved, debauched, wicked, and immoral enemy. As we read through Stefan's anguish, we can feel his turmoil of flesh against spirit, his battle to contend for the faith, his desire to hold onto his faith through his suffering, and his determination to overcome.

After I read an article about Oswiecim in Poland (Auschwitz in German), I was inspired to do this spiritual, historical, fiction story. It came about as I meditated on the continuous negativity and apparent denial of the Holocaust ever happening, what I'm hearing and witnessing in our government, and the ignorance demonstrated in some Christians.

I was astounded by the persistent anti-Semitic sentiment that is prevalent worldwide. Any time racism and bigotry raise its ugly head, evil always pursues. I believe that socialism, communism, etc.

are of the same evil as that of the Nazi Party. All are deceitful lies that promise the sky and deliver famine, disaster, and ruin to the majority of the people. Only the ruling class are benefitted.

As I became aware of the false information and discrimination, my spirit was grieved. It's almost bizarre that people could believe such propaganda when history proves otherwise. The enduring hatred of Jews is so unfounded. As Christians, how can we claim to believe in Jesus and hate the race of people through whom God chose to bring forth his birth?

Yet, the hatred of any group because it differs from what we believe is unfounded. Again the root cause to any unbridled bigotry is self-love. Our self-obsession will not tolerate others opposing our beliefs, what we want, etc. I will endeavor to bring this truth forward more as we progress.

I believe if we forget history, we'll not recognize when it tries to repeat itself. Ignorance to the resurgence of what destroyed other countries will cause us to be overcome by the same evils. There is no new type of socialism that can be good. Socialism or the repression of its people is always the same. That would be like claiming there's a new wickedness that can be good.

This story brings forth a young Polish man falsely accused by the Nazi's, his imprisonment in a Polish prison, and then Auschwitz concentration camp. However, in reality, he probably wouldn't have lived longer than a few months. But the point of this book is to bring forth man's unbridled bigotry, its cruelty to humanity, the holocaust is the result of man's self-love, and to reveal the battle to keep the faith that rages within.

I implore God's soldiers to comprehend the conflict between flesh and spirit that we face whenever we find ourselves in unjust situations. Stefan reveals that we have two choices when faced with horrendous trials, storms, obstacles, etc. in life. We either become negative, murmur, complain, and blame God for our circumstance, or we use the situation as an opportunity to help others and overcome by faith as the early church.

Furthermore, I was compelled to write this book because of what has become more and more evident with some in our government. I felt the need to assist people in recognizing the dangers of socialism and communism. I believe there is not much difference between the two. Under communism there is no such thing as private property; it is state owned. Under socialism there is private property to an extent, but all industrial and production capacity is managed by the government. Examples of socialist system of government are the former Soviet Union, Cuba, Venezuela, etc.

In our government, we have some who are as artful, cunning, crafty, and deceitful as Hitler in propagating socialism in our country. In other words, they have an uncanny ability to make socialism appear to be a wonderful thing. Yet, the people listening are so mesmerized that they disregard the poverty and hardship of those who actually live in a socialist country.

The objective of this book mixed with facts and fiction is to cause Christians and Patriots to realize the appeasement mentality of what will be will be is playing into the hands of those endeavoring to destroy the foundational truths of this country, take away the voice of "We the People," and make the government the ruling power (which is socialism or communism). Before we awaken in a nightmare of either socialism, communism, or sharia law, we must vote these anti-God, anti-Christian, and anti-Constitution government officials out of office.

I am not propagating a hate message against those trying to destroy our Capitalist nation, our Constitution, or that America is a Christian nation. What I am trying to do is awaken us to what will happen if these people keep holding office.

Although this is fact and fiction, its truths cannot be overlooked. We are daily confronted with an enemy who is trying to destroy our faith in Christ. I encourage all who read about Stefan and his turmoil of spirit in such an horrific situation, to be encouraged that we can do all things through Christ which strengtheneth us during the most vicious storm, the most gigantic obstacle, and Satan's most diabolical strategy!

Prologue

"History is the witness of the times, the torch of truth, the life of memory, the teacher of life, the messenger of antiquity."

—Cicero

Prologue

SECTION I

"Anti-Semitism is a noxious weed that should
be cut out. It has no place in America."

—William Howard Taft

Antisemitism

ANTISEMITISM IS DEFINED AS hostility toward or discrimination against Jews as a religious, ethnic, or racial group. It's a bigoted sowing of distrust and spreading of harmful ideas. It claims the Jews are traitors who are undermining our country. False reports allege Jews control the media, banks, government, and are behind the scenes furthering their plans of world domination.

Despite historical facts, holocaust denial spreads the false idea that Jews invented or exaggerated the holocaust, including the diary of Anne Frank. Furthermore, antisemitism denies the massacre of Jews, the use of gas chambers in concentration camps, and the murder of millions of Jews during World War II.

Although we are aware of antisemitism, do we really comprehend its evil? Do we really understand it's hostility, aggression, or enmity towards Jews as a religion or as a social minority? This enmity is a biased prejudice against Jews founded upon false beliefs.

Let me explain what I mean by false beliefs. First of all, the hatred of Jews is rooted in lies that they are the cause of all problems befalling mankind. Secondly, antisemitism sentiment began in the early church that claimed the Jews rejected and killed Christ. This hostility has continued right up to today with Christians blaming the Jews for the death of Jesus and calling them "Christ killers" and "Devils." Such ignorance is unacceptable in any of us who claim to be a Christian. Scripture makes clear that "SIN" is what killed Jesus.

Whether we are Jew or Gentile, we must realize, "my sin" is what caused his death. Yes, it was our sins that nailed him to the cross, but it was God's love for us that induced him to suffer on the cross.

Antisemitism raises its ugly intolerance wherever Jews have settled outside of Palestine. No matter where we look in history, there has always been a depraved hatred of Jews. We would think that after the Holocaust and its murderous rage by the Nazis of over 6 million Jews, there would be an abhorrence to antisemitism. However, in the United States, it seems the hatred is rising at an alarming rate today especially in California, New York, New Jersey, and Massachusetts that have the highest Jewish population.

On October 27, 2019, there was the slaughter of eleven and injuring of six Jewish members of the Pittsburgh's Tree of Life synagogue. The man who committed the crime told the police that he wanted all Jews to die. As this evil is raising its ugly head, we are reminded of Hitler, the Nazis, and the Holocaust.

In December of 2019 in midtown Manhattan, a sixty-five year old Jewish man was punched and kicked by a twenty-eight-year-old man who was yelling antisemitic insults. Then a thirty-four-year-old Orthodox woman was walking with her three-year-old son in Brooklyn, when she was approached from behind and whacked in the head by a woman shouting racial slurs.

In New York, a man burst into a Hanukkah party stabbing five people. Then during a recent Passover observance, a gunman murdered a Jewish worshiper and wounded three others at a house of worship in Poway, California. Then in a kosher supermarket in December of 2019, a man and woman went on a furious rampage killing three people.

Although antisemitism has been around since Bible times, it reached a racial dimension unheard of before the Nazis. The Nazi Party regarded the Jews as a subhuman race and a dangerous cancer that would destroy the German people. Such evil is brought about through the self-love of those who believe they are superior.

The antisemitism brutality unleashed by Nazi Germany under the leadership of Adolf Hitler from 1933 to 1945 sought the "final solution to the Jewish question." This scheme involved the murder of all Jews whether man, woman, or child. Nazis would settle for nothing less than the eradication of Jews from the human race.

To the Nazis, the extinction of the Jews was crucial to the purification and even the salvation of the German people. Nazi self-obsession with racial purity believed the *Aryan* race or the German race, who were superior to all other races, had a duty to control the world. This supremacy appealed both to the multitudes and to the economic elites.

Because of its wide spread acceptance in Germany, antisemitism became the official government philosophy. It was taught in the schools, elaborated in "scientific" journals, and promoted by a vast, highly efficient organization for global propaganda or deception.

Under Hitler, the liquidation of European Jewry became the official party policy in 1941. This strategy was responsible for an estimated 6 million Jews being exterminated. During the Holocaust of World War II, death camps such as Auschwitz, Chelmno, Belzec, and Treblinka, were the instruments whereby Jews were exterminated by gas chambers, starvation, or being worked to death.

First Letter

Dear Mama,

I was arrested at work on some political charge. A couple of guys who weren't dressed as police arrested me. Because of Uncle Blasej teaching us some German, I heard one of them refer to me as a filthy Slav. Other than that, the facts are unclear, and I have no idea what I did. But you've always taught me that truth must stand on its principle and not waiver in its belief.

In the interim, I'll keep my spirits up with your smile. Your picture is such an encouragement to me. It's like I can hear you giving me a scripture to stay the course.

Mama, I thank you for bringing me up in the love and nurture of the Lord. It seems as though my faith is confronted with an unknown storm. To be arrested and placed behind bars for no crime is an incredible obstacle to overcome. But I know the Lord will never leave me nor forsake me.

I thank the Lord for Aunt Helena who sends us the updates on Smith Wigglesworth's preaching from America. It was such a joy when she paid our passage to visit her in California, and we heard him preach at the Gospel Tabernacle in October 1922. I was only twelve, but my memory is emblazoned with you entering with consumption and leaving healed. It was an incredible experience that still fills me with its joy.

I trust my faith will keep me steadfast during this ridiculous ordeal. My boss knows that I was arrested, so I'm sure my job will be waiting when I'm released.

It's so confusing with the constant interrogations. I'm being treated like a criminal, but I have no idea what they're trying to find out. The whole thing is like a bad dream, of which, I pray I awaken from soon.

Well, Mama, it seems I will miss Nadzia's birthday. But she knows her loving brother will make it up to her, when I can.

Tell cousin Radoslaw that I'll have to forego our game until further notice.

Give my love to Papa.

Your loving son,

Stefan

P. S. I keep hearing in my heart that if ye suffer for righteousness' sake, happy are ye, and be not afraid of their terror, neither be troubled. It's a comforting verse, but it does cause me to question what the Lord is preparing me for.

MISTAKE

An error in judgment, a misunderstanding,
Wrong comprehension, facts distorted.
Hope, sees rectification, waiting to hear,
Wrong guy arrested.

It's a terrible error, given a full apology,
Sincere regret for frustration.
Income forfeited, family visitation prohibited,
Merciless interrogation.

People are capable of making mistakes,
Not flawless and perfect creatures.
Errors and mistakes are part of Humanity,
That's for sure.

Adolf Hitler

ADOLF HITLER WAS BORN on April 20,1889 in Austria which was, at that time, part of Austria-Hungary. Because he was an angry, temperamental, slothful, unhappy child with an unpredictable temperament, he held a deep resentment towards his strict father. His laziness carried over to his schooling where he never advanced beyond a secondary education and left school at the age of sixteen with the dream of becoming a painter.

In 1907, he left home for Vienna where he lived a vagabond existence. He survived from hand to mouth on occasional odd jobs and selling watercolor scenes of Vienna. It was during this time, that he gained his pathological hatred of Jews, Marxists, and the Habsburg monarchy.

In Vienna, he picked up the obsession of antisemitism with its cruel results. His self-centeredness and concern with the "purity of blood" ruled every aspect of his being that remained with him to the end of his life. To Hitler, the Jews were the cause of all the turmoil, degeneracy, and destruction in culture, politics, the economy, etc. He felt they were sub-humans who were devastating all facets of life. If not stopped, the Jews would destroy the purity of the *Aryan* race.

Hitler advocated the concept of a biologically superior *Aryan* or Germanic master race of strong, tall, blond-haired, blue-eyed pure-blood supermen. The Nazis sought to breed such men through the "Lebensborn" program with the goal to raise the birth rate of

Aryan children of persons classified as "racially pure" and "healthy" based on Nazi racial hygiene and health ideology. Ironically, Hitler only shared the blue-eye characteristic. Otherwise, he was a 5' 9" tall, brown haired, 155 pound Austrian.

He was obsessed with the idea of inequality among the races, nations, and individuals as part of an unalterable natural order that promoted the "Aryan race" as the creative component of mankind. As far as Hitler was concerned the natural unit of mankind was the people to whom the German people was the ultimate or the exclusive race. All others were inferior or substandard.

It was Hitler who gave the Nazi Party its swastika which became a symbol of pure evil. Because he comprehended the significance of language, propaganda played a major role in his rise to power. He was a master of deceit and with his powerful talent as an orator, he seemed to mesmerize his listeners with his gruff voice, his pompous, sullen speeches, and his gift for self-dramatization.

The people were desiring a better life and believed Hitler was the one to give it to them. However, Hitler's Third Reich was entirely fascist (a political philosophy, movement, or regime that exalts nation and often race above the individual and stands for centralized autocratic government headed by a dictatorial leader and forcible suppression of opposition). Within a couple of months of Hitler rising to power, he achieved complete dictatorial control making Germany a one political party country.

As the leader of the Nazi Party and as Fuhrer, Hitler sought "living space" for the German people in Eastern Europe. Because of his devotion to dominate Europe, he ordered the invasion of Poland on September 1, 1939. This maneuver resulted in Britain and France declaring war on Germany and initiating World War II in Europe.

Hitler strongly believed that the Jews were the enemy of the German people. In January 1942, he had decided that Jews, Slavs, and others considered undesirable were to be eliminated. This genocide was organized and executed by Heinrich Himmler and Reinhard Heydrich.

Hitler was convinced that Germany would only regain her health by eliminating the Jews. He had also declared the easiest way to quickly pacify the areas would be best achieved by "shooting anyone who looked odd."

The Nazi regime, under Hitler's leadership, a racially inspired ideology, was responsible for the extermination of at least six million Jews and other victims whom he and his followers viewed as subhuman or socially detrimental. Altogether, Hitler and the Nazis were responsible for the genocide of about 19.3 million civilians and prisoners of war, 28.7 million soldiers and civilians died as a result of military action in the European theater. World War II represented the deadliest war in history.

According to a U. S. Office of Strategic Services (OSS) report, "The Nazi Master Plan," Hitler's plan was to annihilate all influence of Christian churches within the Reich. He eventually planned the total eradication of Christianity. Although this goal was an element to his movement, Hitler saw it as unwise to publicly express this extreme position. He intended to wait until after the war before implementing this plan.

After January 1945, Hitler accepted the inevitability of defeat and never left the Chancellery or its bunker. As Soviet forces approached Berlin in late April 1945, Hitler began to contemplate suicide.

On April 29, 1945, he married his mistress Eva Braun in a small civil ceremony within the Fuhrerbunker, an air raid shelter located near the Reich Chancellery in Berlin, Germany. After the wedding, he dictated his final political testament charging the leaders of the nation to carry out merciless opposition to international Jewry.

Then on April 30, 1945, Hitler is believed to have shot himself in the head. Following him in death, Eva took cyanide poisoning. His body and that of his wife were carried into the garden of the Reich Chancellery by aides, covered with petrol and burned according to Hitler's instructions.

Hitler's final morbid act of self-destruction aptly symbolized the career of a political leader whose main legacy to Europe was the destruction of its civilization and the senseless sacrifice of human life. In his self-love, he ruthlessly pursued his quest for self-satisfaction and power. Hitler's hate, bigotry, and self-love harvested a Holocaust of pure evil against humanity.

Second Letter

Dear Mama,

Cousin Radoslaw is here with me. He was arrested last week. Again, an arrest takes place, and the reason is political without any evidence of a crime.

We now know that our charges stem from the Nazi control of Poland. They're accusing us of being antagonists to their policy, because we're against repressing any man on the basis of race, color, or creed. As Christians, we believe the Scriptures that acclaim all men are created equal, for there is neither Jew nor Greek, there is neither bond nor free, there is neither male nor female: for ye are all one in Christ Jesus.

I don't want to frighten you, but rumors constantly affirm that Auschwitz is our next home. Word through the grapevine claims it's inevitable. The Nazis will have no interference with their hatred for the Jewish people and any they believe to be inferior. Their self-love has created beings with no compassion for humanity other than those they consider worthy.

Yet again, I think of what Smith Wigglesworth said about the opportunity being all around. The needy are everywhere—begin. I wonder if I'm here to encourage others in the faith. I've been reminding all who will listen about the early church. If those believers could endure such cruelty at the hands of man, we can do likewise through faith.

Mama, I've been meditating on the dream I had at sixteen where a voice told me to remain unmarried like the Apostle Paul. I keep wondering if that's why Marta died before I asked her to marry me. The dream never made sense. After all, I'm not an apostle, evangelist, or any minister. But, Mama, I must confess that since I've been arrested, I've felt like a preacher. Before this, I never thought of anything except being a mason. After all, I've been one since I was fourteen. Anyway, I believe the Lord has impressed me of the further heartbreak that would have occurred if I had married.

I must admit it's difficult to overcome by faith with the cruel interrogations. We've committed no crime, yet they accuse us of being evil antagonists because of our beliefs. It's extremely trying at times to be imprisoned for political reasons, when we've done no wrong.

The Holy Spirit reminded me of the cruelty that Jesus suffered for doing nothing wrong. I may not have done anything politically wrong that I know of, but I can't claim that I've done no wrong. God knows I've had to ask for forgiveness almost daily in here.

I forgot to tell you, but Radoslaw and I believe we know what happened. There was a man who had come to our workplace at different times, and asked us separately what we thought of the Jews. Both I and Radoslaw said we had some Jewish friends who own a local restaurant where we often have lunch. The man smiled and said that was interesting. Radoslaw described the same man that had asked me that question a few days before him.

We're sure of it, because a couple of days after the man visited me at work, I was arrested. Then the next day after Radoslaw was visited, he was arrested. He must have been a Nazi trying to find those who were not anti-Semites. However, I've also heard they want to eradicate Slavs. In my first letter, I told you I was called a filthy Slav when arrested.

Anyway, I try to encourage Radoslaw and the rest as best I can. Besides, I would think a civilized world will intervene shortly. Surely, the Christian world has not become deceived by the propaganda of Nazism.

I hope your birthday was a pleasant one.

Your loving son,

Stefan

P. S. The Holy Spirit has encouraged that I can do all things through Christ which strengtheneth me. I believe, as the early Church was persecuted for their faith, the Lord is preparing me for a storm of suffering. I pray I can overcome whatever is ahead through the grace of God.

VACILLATION

Blackness, dark as the night,
Confuses my stability, despairing thoughts,
Run rampant through my mind.

Mental faculty, all sensibility,
Flung to and fro, a leaf hurled in the wind,
Questions upon questions unanswered.

Day is overcome, night fears,
Ground shifts like quicksand,
Faith becomes confused.

Conviction fluctuates,
Doubt grips like an iron fist,
I shouldn't be caged in iron bars.

Mama's smile glares through,
Light of faith springs forth,
Bringing memories– awakening.

Bigotry responsible,
Jesus suffered persecution,
So will his disciples.

SECTION II

"Let Him lead thee blindfold onwards,
Love needs not to know;
Children whom the Father leadeth
Ask not where they go,
Though the path be all unknown,
Over moors and mountains lone."
—Gerhard Tersteegen (The Blessed Journey)

The Nazi Party

THE NATIONAL SOCIALIST GERMAN Workers' Party, generally referred to as the Nazi Party, was a political party in Germany and active between 1920 and 1945. It was created by a Munich Locksmith in 1919. The Nazi Party not only created, but supported the ideology of National Socialism.

Through the Nazi Party Hitler exploited his racist world view. He believed that people could be separated into a hierarchy of different races where some were outstanding, and others were substandard. As far as Hitler was concerned, the German or *Aryan* race was the superior and indisputably enhanced race.

Under Hitler the Nazi Party grew steadily in its home base of Bavaria. It grew partly through Hitler's oratorical skills, partly through the SA's (Sturmabteilung) appeal to unemployed young men, and partly because there was a backlash against socialist and liberal politics in Bavaria as Germany's economic problems deepened.

Because Hitler was a decorated frontline veteran, the Nazi Party was appealing to World War I veterans, as well as small businessmen and disillusioned former members of rival parties. Nazi rallies were held in beer halls, where oppressed men could get free beer. Oppression and intoxication together united these men to believe in Hitler's propaganda.

Emerging from the German nationalist and populist *Free Corps* that fought as mercenary or private armies, the party was created to draw workers away from communism into nationalism. Initially, the Nazi political strategy was anti-big business and anti-capitalist rhetoric. However, it was later downplayed to gain the support of business leaders, and in the 1930's, the party's central focus shifted to antisemitic and anti-Marxist ideas.

The party aimed to unify "racially desirable" Germans as national comrades, while rejecting those considered to be political dissidents, physically or intellectually substandard, or of a foreign race. The Nazis pursued the strengthening of the Germanic people (the *Aryan* master race) through racial purity and eugenics (the science of improving a human population by controlled breeding to increase the occurrence of desirable hereditary characteristics).

In order to safeguard the supposed purity and strength of the *Aryan* race, the Nazis sought to exterminate Jews, Romani, Poles, and most other Slavs, along with the physically and mentally handicapped, Africans, Jehovah Witnesses, and political opponents.

Nazi Germany was authoritarian, ultra-nationalism, characterized by dictatorial power, and forcible suppression of opposition. The Nazi Party's oppression reached its pinnacle when the party-controlled German state set in motion the *Final Solution* to eliminate Jewry from Europe. This resulted in the genocide of six million Jews and millions of other targeted victims known as the Holocaust.

Third Letter

Dear Mama,

Today, I am twenty-nine years old, and I can sense your birthday prayers for me. I feel as though I have aged in the knowledge of someone with grey hair. The Lord has caused me to become like a wise old man in such a short time.

You see, Radoslaw and I are now at Auschwitz concentration camp. What to believe is a daily confusion to us. The commandant, Rudolf Hoess, placed the words, *Arbeit Macht Frei* which means "work sets you free" over the gate that greeted us when we arrived. We have always been hard working masons. But to hope that work will set us free in these conditions seems pointless.

I keep praying for grace to overcome. I must admit at times, I find myself feeling not so wise and praying for grace to be enabled to do all things through Christ which strengtheneth me. Then, I find myself encouraging others and getting through another day.

I know the only reason we are still alive is that we are able bodied workers. However, it's difficult working in the manufacturing of synthetic rubber as slave labor. We are forced to work with little food, little sleep, and our clothes are turning into rags on our back. Yet, by the grace of God, we are still here and able to work.

My mind keeps hearing the hymn by Gerhard Tersteegen called *The Blessed Journey* that love needs not to know where the

Father leadeth. It is difficult at times to go on through this unknown path, but I love Jesus, and I know he loves me.

God has used us to bring Jesus to some and that does give us joy amongst all this grief. I've led several to faith in Christ who were on the verge of death from the abuse. I'm reminded of the thief on the cross who called out to Jesus at the last moment, and the Lord told him he'd be in paradise that day.

There seems to be the hope that the allies will rescue us. We've heard rumors that they are close. The sound of bombing is heard in the distance, but the cruelty goes on day after day.

Please continue to pray for me and Radoslaw. He has come a long way in the faith since we arrived here. Just the other day, he led someone to Jesus. It seemed to put a spring in his walk after.

I miss you, Papa, and Nadzia. How I miss your cooking, my warm bed, and your nightly Bible reading.

Your loving son,

Stefan

P. S. They took your picture when I arrived.

MOTHER'S BOUQUET

Happy place, sustained by love,
Peaceful environment, an ocean's calm,
Not rich, but all needs supplied,
Mama's hands nurture with care, homemade clothes,
Vogue and flawless, above store bought.
Childhood memories linger– a fragrant flower.

My bed, snuggly warm, sheets fresh and clean,
Morning's light, clothes laid out, washed and ironed,
Smell the baking rolls, use lots of honey, cup of hot tea,
Off to school, nice and full, life is splendid,
Home again, smell the cookies baking.
Childhood memories linger– a fragrant flower.

Mama sets the table humming a hymn,
A warm embrace, family cherished, priceless jewels,
Everyone happy, blithe, Mama tends to all needs,
Gone with a blink of time, gaiety is cloaked in bleakness,
Auschwitz supplants the nurtured household.
Childhood memories fragment– a fading flower.

Nazism

NAZISM IS THE BODY of political and economic creeds held and put into effect by the Nazis in Germany from 1933 to 1945. It included the dictatorial principle of government, predominance of especially Germanic groups who were believed to be racially superior, and the supremacy of the Fuhrer.

It's a form of fascism (a system of government that is a type of one-party dictatorship that puts nation and often a race of people above the individual) and showed that ideology's contempt for liberal democracy (this is not the liberal democrats of America, but a democracy with protection for individual liberty and property by rule of law) and the parliamentary system (a system where the executive branch of government has the direct or indirect support of the parliament), but also incorporated fervent antisemitism (hostility or prejudice against Jews), anti-communism (a political movement and ideology opposed to communism), scientific racism (a belief that experiential evidence exists to support or justify racial discrimination, racial inferiority, or racial superiority), and eugenics (the science of improving population by controlled breeding to increase the occurrence of desirable heritable characteristics) into its creed.

The origins of Nazism can be traced to the Prussian tradition that was established under Frederick William I, Frederick the Great, and Otto von Bismarck who viewed the militant spirit and the discipline of the Prussian army as the standard for all individual and civic life.

Not only was Hitler influenced during his youth by the trends in the German tradition, but he was influenced by specific Austrian movements professing various political thoughts of domination and antisemitism. Hitler had a ferocious nationalism that incorporated a contempt for Slavs and a hatred for Jews. Perhaps this disdain can be traced to his bitter experiences as an unsuccessful artist living hand to mouth on the streets of Vienna.

The defeat on World War I triggered a surge in the growth of Nazism in Germany. The country's disenchantment, pauperization, and annoyance especially in the middle classes, smoothed the way for Hitler and the Nazi Party's propaganda or misinformation.

It was Hitler's belief that all propaganda must hold its intellectual level at the capability of the least intelligent of those to whom it is targeted and that its truthfulness is much less essential than success. He cared not about veracity, but whatever it took to persuade his audience to believe what he said. Hitler's charismatic personality seemed to mesmerize his listeners to follow blindly whatever he propagated.

This blind obedience quickly spread Nazism and the magnitude of the Nazi Party. Although Nazism held economic and political success, its power was maintained by coercion and mass manipulation. The regime circulated a constant deluge of propaganda through its rallies, especially its elaborately staged Nuremberg rallies, its insignia, and its uniformed troops were created to influence a sense of omnipotence. However, the base of its propaganda machine was its method of terror, with its pervasive secret police and concentration camps.

Nazism fueled and centered on antisemitism to make the Jews a representation of all that was detested and feared. Through deceitful rhetoric, the Nazi Party depicted the Jews as the enemy of all classes of society. In short, Nazism was a self-centered love and belief that the German people were the superior race and all others were to be in subjection or eliminated. This obsession reaped an unbridled bigotry and hatred determined to exterminate Jewry from the face of the earth.

The SS (uniformed police force of the Nazi Party) was the main tool of control to bring about unification. This union was instituted at any cost to lives. All resistance to the party was destroyed either by absolute terror, or by the inclusive fear of potential suppression. Any challengers of the regime were labeled enemies of the state and of the people. Through an intricate network of informers, who were often members of the family or friends, people were compelled to use the utmost caution on all they said and did. All words and all actions were monitored by those trying to gain favor with the Nazi Party.

Along with the debauched methods of the normal judicial process, special detention camps were constructed. The SS exerted absolute authority and instituted a system of fiendish brutality unequaled in modern times. What occurred in the camps is a horror show of the results of unbridled bigotry.

Under Adolf Hitler, Nazism was a belief observed with steadfast commitment by not only Germans, but those who were close allies to this fanatical system. Under the supremacy of the Nazi Party or Third Reich, the Jews, political opponents, and other undesirables were excluded, incarcerated, or executed. Millions of people were eventually annihilated in a genocide that became known as the Holocaust during World War II. Included in those millions was the extermination of two-thirds of the Jewish population in Europe.

Fourth Letter

Dear Mama,

Time crawls, and the cruelty seems to be magnified daily. We're hungry, thirsty, pestilence abounds, and we have little sleep. Sanitation seems to be a byword, as we live in filth and disgrace.

God gave us a free-will, but the Nazis believe their will is supreme. They are cruel and heartless task masters who consider all who are not German as expendable. We are treated as subhuman and have no place in humanity. However, Radoslaw and I know that God sees us as his sons, and we look forward to that city which hath foundations whose builder and maker is God.

I struggle to see your smile. When it breaks through, I feel such comfort.

My mind hears you reading the Scriptures. Lately, it's always that with Christ all things are possible.

I remind myself, Radoslaw, and all who will listen that we can do all things through Christ which strengtheneth us. If the early church could face the lions, torture, being burned on a stake, etc., we must hold fast to God's love and overcome by faith in God whose grace is sufficient.

Paul struggled with his thorn in the flesh, but the Lord told him that his grace was sufficient. I believe Jesus was telling him that through the grace of God, all things are possible. We can overcome any thorn in our flesh through God's grace. It's like Jacob wrestling all night with the angel of the Lord to keep his flesh under. I must admit that I have to wrestle with my flesh to deny its tendency to doubt and questions. But I've determined to keep my flesh crucified and trust that God has all things in control.

Tell Papa I didn't forget his birthday.

I send my love to all.

Your loving son,

Stefan

P. S. I keep remembering Smith Wigglesworth's words: "There is power to overcome everything in the world through the name of Jesus." I wrestle day and night to hang onto that truth. I've determined to hold onto Christ even if the hollow of my thigh is put out of joint. It will be extremely painful, but my goal is to come out of this evil storm of hate and bigotry and be blessed.

THE SONG OF THE WIND

Listen to the song of the wind,
Howling throughout the earth.
Does it sing of merriment?
Is it merely the rustling of leaves?
Maybe it breathes of melancholy. Perhaps,
It's really a wailing song of creation.

Whether the wind blows, north, turns south,
Heads east or west, there's no escape
From man's inhumane bigotry.
It hears man's debased cruelty,
The sights it sees daily of,
Men, women, and children slaughtered as cattle.

No matter where it journeys,
It espies mankind destroying itself through selfishness.
A madman lets loose his rage against mankind
—the innocent lay dead.
A racist decides to eliminate those he deems inferior
—millions are slaughtered to satisfy his hatred.

Prejudice rages its ugly face.
Some think it's an angel of light.
What light is in the destruction of man?
Don't all have the same Creator?
Don't all have the breath of life?
Is blood other than red?

SECTION II

Listen to the song of the wind,
As it continuously resonates,
A weeping melody of woe.
There's no rejoicing in the keepers of earth,
Turning into barbarians,
And replicating devils.

SECTION III

"We gain strength, and courage, and confidence by each experience in which we really stop to look fear in the face. . . we must do that which we think we cannot."

—ELEANOR ROOSEVELT

The Holocaust

THE HOLOCAUST, ALSO CALLED *Ha-Shoah* in Hebrew, was the genocide of 6 million Jews during World War II (1941 to 1945). The Jews
who died during this time were not casualties of the fighting during
the war, but victims of Germany's premeditated and methodical effort to annihilate the entire Jewish population of Europe. This plan
was called the "Final Solution" by Hitler and those who carried out
the extermination.

The antisemitism belief by the Nazis was no secret, for in
1919, Adolf Hitler had written of the necessity to remove the Jews
altogether. He propagated the Jews as an evil race who were after
world domination. To the Nazis, the Jews were not seen as a religious group, but a dangerous race that was detrimental to the health
of the German people.

As far as the Nazis were concerned, the *Aryans* or the German people were the superior race. All others were considered as
subhuman and expendable. To justify their treatment of Jews, the
Nazis combined their racial theories with the evolutionary theories of Charles Darwin. It only made sense that since the Germans
were the strongest and fittest of humanity, they were destined to
rule. Whereas, the weak and racially polluted Jews were destined
to extinction.

Because Hitler viewed the Jews as racial polluters, a cancer on
German society, he began to restrict the Jews with legislation and

terror, which involved burning books written by Jews, expelling them from their professions and public schools, seizing their businesses and property, and prohibiting them from attending public events.

Hitler resisted Jews for the values they brought into the world. Social justice and compassionate assistance to the weak stood in the way of what he perceived as the natural order. He believed the powerful are to exert unrestrained power, and the restraint of the implementation of power would inevitably lead to the declining and eventual defeat of the master race.

In 1941, Germany began the "Final Solution" by forming four mobile paramilitary death squads who gathered Jews town by town, marched them to massive pits dug earlier, stripped them, lined them up, and shot them with automatic weapons. The dead or dying would fall into the pits to be buried in mass graves. History estimates that by the end of 1942, those death squads had murdered more than 1.3 million Jews.

The Nazis, in the Spring of 1942, built six killing centers or death camps in occupied Poland that would be the essential instrument of the "final solution." Before the camps, the death squads had to travel to kill their victims. The killing centers reversed the process by bringing the victims by train, often in cattle cars, to their killers.

These concentration camps of Chelmno, Belzec, Sobibor, Treblinka, Majdanek, and Auschwitz-Birkenau were located near railway lines and made the daily transportation of Jews an easy endeavor. The purpose of the camps varied from slave labor camps, transit camps, concentration camps, and the infamous death camps. Whatever their purpose, all camps involved unbearable malice.

The extermination camps became factories generating corpses at minimal physical and emotional harm to the German staffs. With the assistance of Ukrainian and Latvian collaborators and prisoners, tens of thousands of prisoners could be killed each month by a few Germans.

At Chelmno, the first extermination camp, the Nazis utilized mobile gas vans. Permanent gas chambers linked to the crematoria where the bodies were burned were built to expedite the killings. Carbon monoxide was the gas of choice at most camps, but

Zyklon-B, a lethal killing agent of hydrogen cyanide, used in pesticide, was utilized primarily at Auschwitz.

During the course of German-occupied territory, the state of the Jews was wretched. They had measly resources, few allies, and encountered difficult options. A few people came to their rescue, often at the risk of their own lives. This reality is seen in the *Hiding Place* by Corrie ten Boom and what happened to her and her family for protecting Jews.

To all who understand the Holocaust, it is perceived as the illustrative expression of uncontrolled evil. It portrayed man's self-love and his prejudice of fellow humanity. In its delineation is a constant reminder that unbridled bigotry, not nipped in the bud, will harvest evil in an uncontrollable magnitude.

Fifth Letter

Dear Mama,

Radoslaw is weakening under the hard work, lack of rest, continual hunger, cold, filth, and cruelty. But he still does his daily work. He says, he knows it's the grace of God that gets him through. If the guards think a prisoner is unfit to work, the prisoner is eliminated on the spot. I believe they do that in front us to cause fear. However, we are not afraid of dying. Our goal is to run our race until God says our time is up.

What I've heard about the treatment of the Jews is worse, The tales to my ears are horror upon horror. It's supposed be the *Final Solution* to the Jewish problem. I don't really grasp what the problem is about. All I know is that we are to pray for Israel. The Nazis must be unbelievers.

What I've heard is horrific. The Nazis used trucks made into a mobile gas chamber. The exhaust fumes then murder Jews, whose bodies are then disposed of in crematoriums or a structure where the bodies are burned.

The truth of the horrors here cannot be overemphasized. Mama, the unbridled bigotry is a nightmare. It's like Hitler is a madman running loose on a murderous rampage and no one is stopping him. His henchmen are as heartless as him for carrying out his orders. It's as if they are void of a conscience. They are pure evil hiding in skin.

The Holy Spirit continuously reminds me of the cross and what Jesus suffered for me, and that his disciples will be persecuted also. He affirms that nothing can separate me from the love of God in Christ Jesus. As I wrote that, his love engulfed me and humbled me.

I keep telling Radoslaw to be absent from the body is to be present with the Lord. He smiles and shakes his head.

Your loving son,

Stefan

P. S. Radoslaw thinks I'm silly for writing letters to myself. He doesn't understand that it helps me remember you and the strength of your faith.

A HEART TO GIVE

Why does man take life so easily,
Without thought to his callous deeds,
Never understanding life's value,
Satisfying debauchery at any cost?
Man kills without remorse.
Man hates without conviction.
Lover of self at the expense of life,
And self-indulgence takes dominance.

The good Samaritan came to give life,
His thoughts centered on man's necessity,
Was never concerned about himself,
His heart ached for man's welfare.
Self-love was not in his vocabulary,
He had no earthly place to lay his head.
The man ought to have been venerated,
Perhaps won the Nobel Peace prize.

Men convinced that he opposed their freedom,
Tortured him to forbid his interference.
He declared he'd come for their redemption,
Because love brought him into this world.
They pierced him through and laughed,
"He can't give life to himself."
Why does man take life so easily,
Without thought to his callous deeds?

Auschwitz Concentration Camp

Auschwitz was Nazi Germany's largest concentration and extermination camp. As the most infamous and deadly of the concentration camps, it was actually three camps in one consisting of a prison camp (Auschwitz I), an extermination camp (Auschwitz II-Birkenau), and a slave labor camp (Auschwitz III-Buna-Monowitz).

As the Jewish prisoners arrived at Auschwitz, they faced *Selektion* (the sorting of deportees or prisoners into two groups: either those to do forced labor or those to be killed). Pregnant women, young children, the elderly, handicapped, sick, and infirm were selected by a German doctor for immediate death in gas chambers. Whereas, able-bodied prisoners were chosen for forced labor in the factories, such as IG Farben, that were neighboring Auschwitz.

Because of the intense atrocities that took place in Auschwitz, it has become the emblematic site of the "final solution," and the symbolic center of the Holocaust. It's reported that between 1.1 and 1.5 million people died there. Of that number, 90 percent were Jews.

With its dominant location in the European railway system, Auschwitz was located at a railway junction with rail lines that were used to transport Jews from throughout Europe to their death. In its use of gas chambers, it uncovered the thought-out nature of the annihilation of which it became a center.

When entering the camp, the words *Arbeit Macht Frei* (work will set you free) were inscribed above the gate. The only ones with freedom were the captors, who had the freedom to kill, to torture, and to maim. This motto was, in fact, anything but true to those who entered through those gates as prisoners. It gave false hope to the Polish prisoners who could never be part of the German community. In reality, Auschwitz was a closed area in which its prisoners had no rights at all.

Inmates struggled to live each day on a starvation diet, deprived of warm clothes or shoes, with modicum sleep, no privacy, subject to a tyrannical regime imposed by the SS and prisoner *Kapos* (prisoners who were assigned to supervise forced labor or carry out administrative tasks), and exhausted by the daily twelve hours of rigid exertion.

Because of the high death rate at Auschwitz, the crematorium was needed to dispose of corpses. However, the camp slowly became part of the Nazis' genocidal system to annihilate the Jewish population in Europe. With the gas chamber in place, the Auschwitz crematorium became a small but efficient death machine capable of killing and incineration facilities under one roof.

Jews who arrived with their families were torn from them during selection, and knew that their loved ones had been killed in the gas chambers. They also knew they had been given only a reprieve from death, and every day could be their last. If this devastating emotional burden wasn't enough, their living and working conditions were severe. Considered as subhuman to the Nazis, the debased treatment inflicted upon Jews was not only horrific, but malicious.

Prisoners were given to physicians as guinea pigs. Experiments on camp inmates began at the beginning of the war. Recent medical graduates of the SS medical academy were offered inmates for surgery practice, inmates were injected with live malaria cells. Furthermore, research in Auschwitz concentrated on mass sterilization of able-bodied Jews without impairing their ability to work.

Auschwitz, by the end of the war, had become the most lethal death camp. Of the 1.3 million people deported to the camp, an estimated 1.1 million died. The figures include 74,000 non-Jewish Poles, 21,000 Roma, 15,00 Soviet POW's, and up to 15,000 other Europeans, and about 1 million Jews. Many of those not gassed died of starvation, exhaustion, disease, individual executions, or beatings. Others were killed during medical experiments. Thus, making Auschwitz an evil killing machine of unbridled bigotry. It revealed the steps that self-love will go to eliminate anyone deemed to be inferior to self-love's specifications or beliefs.

Sixth Letter

Dear Mama,

I'm alone. Cousin Radoslaw went home to Jesus a couple of days ago. His body was losing the battle against the abuse, hunger, thirst, etc. The Lord was gracious and took him out of here. He went peacefully during the night. The Nazis didn't have the pleasure of killing him.

This whole situation could be unbelievable, if I were not here. It's heart breaking to know that our blessed country is destroyed by such monstrosities. The Nazis look like humans, but they are beasts clothed as people. They are void of empathy or compassion for any fellow human being they consider as subhuman. I've looked into their eyes to find a sense of concern, but I only see indifference without fellow feeling.

I hear many of the prisoners stating that it cannot go on much longer. They truly believe the allies will end this nightmare soon. I must admit that I've been hoping that since the day Radoslaw and I arrived.

I have often tried to fathom how man can be so cruel to other humans. It seems like they must be possessed of an evil that makes them void of conscience. What I have witnessed has made me want to warn others of what malevolence is harvested from unbridled bigotry. I pray constantly that I will not yield to hate by their malicious cruelty to humanity. Yes, I hate what they are doing, but the Holy Spirit impresses me to see them as man without the love of Jesus.

It is difficult at times under such abuse to think as the Lord wants me to. I pray daily to see them in that manner, but I fail when I witness them murder someone in front of me who has collapsed from exhaustion. I am constantly praying for grace to overcome my flesh and to forgive them as He has forgiven me.

Mama, I try to remember the days of happiness, home, family, etc. Although I must admit that memories are sometimes overshadowed by this cruelty, God's grace always brings a recollection that boosts my faith. He is so faithful to bless me with a memory that takes me out of this place and brings me to happier times.

Your loving son,

Stefan

P. S. The realities of this place are shocking. When I think about everything, it's difficult not to yield to the hopelessness that tries to destroy me at times. The turmoil of my mind and soul is constant. It's a daily conflict of flesh and Spirit, and the inner battle of choice to keep going on can be overwhelming. Thanks be to God for his Holy Spirit. He keeps me afloat with God's promise if I die in this place, I'll be with Jesus.

LIFE'S DECLINE

A dusty road is traveled,
Lungs are filled with toxins,
Each breath is labored–
Demise encumbers about.

Body starts degenerating,
Mind becomes shrouded,
Memories of wellbeing–
Fade like wild flowers.

Running turns to walking,
Steps turn into pain,
Life starts decreasing–
Under the daily struggle.

The soul desires escaping,
From a body's prison walls,
Craves life everlasting–
With the Savior.

SECTION IV

"For I am persuaded, that neither death, nor life, nor angels, nor principalities, nor powers, nor things present, nor things to come, Nor height, nor depth, nor any other creature, shall be able to separate us from the love of God, which is in Christ Jesus our Lord."

—ROMANS 8:38–39

Josef Mengele

Josef Mengele known as the "Angel of Death" was born on March 16, 1911 in Gunzburg Germany and died February 7, 1979. His most famous role was played as the selector on the platform at Auschwitz. There he chose who was to live or who went to the gas chambers.

At the age of twenty, Mengele joined the *Stahlhelm* or Steel Helmet (the largest paramilitary organization). In 1933, he joined the SA and upon being accepted into the Nazi Party in 1937, he applied for membership in the SS.

Mengele chose to concentrate on physical anthropology and genetics in his university studies at the Frankfurt University Institute of Hereditary Biology and Racial Hygiene. An ardent Nazi, he joined the research staff of a newly founded Institute for Hereditary Biology and Racial Hygiene in 1934.

Mengele arrived at Auschwitz on May 30, 1943 as the most diligent and infamous medical researcher. According to Dr. Hans Munch, a colleague of Mengele's at Auschwitz, Mengele entered the camp in a somewhat privileged position. He had been wounded on the Eastern front and was the recipient of an array of medals, including the Iron Cross.

His interests grew out of his work at the Kaiser Wilhelm Institute in Berlin, where he served as research assistant in the study of inherited diseases through research with twins. Mengele believed that comparative autopsies on twins would provide ideal study conditions. However, twins rarely died simultaneously and at a convenient location for the researcher. Auschwitz offered him the opportunity to do what was impossible elsewhere.

Mengele was a very active commandant of the Auschwitz camp. It was the abandoned atmosphere that Mengele thrived. Doctors and prisoners, who testified, indicated he had an omnipresence when the prisoners arrived. His zeal to identify twins on incoming transports prompted him to volunteer regularly to conduct selections. Impeccably dressed in a crisp SS uniform, smiling tightly, his face was the ever present SS physician conducting selections on the arrival ramp. He greeted every incoming train to Auschwitz-Birkenau to make his selections. His riding crop indicated the way, left meant extermination, right meant life.

Beginning in 1944, twins were selected and placed in special blocks in the Gypsy camp where he performed brazen horrific experiments. Twins were marched three times a week to Auschwitz to a big brick building, which resembled a gymnasium. They were kept there for about six to eight hours while sitting naked and being observed by those who took notes. Each body part was studied and photographed. Their heads, arms, and bodies were measured and compared to the other twin. While one twin functioned as the control, the other underwent medical torture.

Mengele was fascinated by eyes and their color. To change the patients eye color, he injected dye into their eyes that resulted in painful infections and sometimes blindness. During his time at Auschwitz, he collected the eyes of his murdered victims. He placed patients in isolation cages and subjected them to a variety of stimuli just to see the reaction. He inoculated with infectious agents to discover the course of infectious disease and resistance to it.

Once he had collected all the data he wanted from a victim, they were killed by a single injection of chloroform in the heart. He took particular care to make sure the twins were murdered at the same time. At which time, dissection of the corpses for final medical analysis was performed, and their organs taken to research centers.

Mengele castrated or sterilized hundreds of male prisoners, the girls were sterilized by burning their uterus. He tossed babies into ovens alive, strapped the breasts with tape after a woman gave birth to see how long it took her unfed infant to die, collected twins, and opened them up with his scalpel to discover the secret of multiple births.

After the war, Mengele went underground, serving for four years as a farm stableman. In 1949, he escaped to South America. He initially lived in and around Buenos Aires, then fled to Paraguay in 1959. While being sought by West Germany, Israel, and Nazi hunters such as *Simon Wiesenthal* who wanted to bring him to trial, he moved to Brazil.

Mengele eluded capture for thirty-four years after the war in spite of extradition requests by the West German government and clandestine operations by the Israeli intelligence agency *Mossad*. On February 7, 1979 while visiting friends in the coastal resort near the Brazilian coast, Mengele suffered a stroke whilst swimming and drowned. He was buried under the false name *Wolfgang Gerhard*. Although his remains were exhumed and positively identified by forensic analysis in 1985, many questioned if it was him. However, in 1992, DNA tests showed conclusively that the remains were that of Josef Mengele.

Seventh Letter

Dear Mama,

Your stocky son is now skin and bones. Radoslaw was a walking stick before his death. If I hadn't known who he was, I wouldn't have recognized him.

Being in this place is a daily nightmare. I keep praying to wake up, but the reality of inhumane cruelty is constant. One of my fellow prisoners told me that one of the SS doctors chose prisoners a couple of days ago from the camp infirmary at Auschwitz I and killed them with phenol heart injections.

I no longer wonder about what is ahead. When the Lord told me not to be afraid of their terror or to be troubled, but be happy to suffer for righteousness' sake, I had no idea it would be so dreadful.

It seems like I'm experiencing what it felt like to the early church to be so persecuted. Disease, death, and vicious cruelty is a daily reality. When I think about the evil that took place at night in the Emperor Nero's imperial gardens. I remember thinking what a monster he was to have Christian men and women covered with pitch, oil, or resin, and nailed to posts of pine, lighted, and then burned as torches for the amusement of the mob. All the while, Nero entertained them in capricious apparel and play acted his art as a charioteer. I do believe the Nazis are even more evil than Nero. He was a madman, but Hitler is worse than that. He is living malice in human form and so is the Nazi Party.

Please pray for me as my faith is challenged continuously, and I'm in a constant battle of my flesh lusting against my spirit. My flesh wants to give into hate, but the Holy Spirit reminds me that I'm only forgiven of my sins as I forgive those who sin against me. Besides, I'm constantly reminded of the glory ahead if I faint not.

Your loving son,

Stefan

P. S. The Holy Spirit keeps reminding me what Smith Wigglesworth said, "The moment a man is born again, he is free and lives in heavenly places. He has no destination except the glory." I strive daily to remember that I'm a pilgrim passing through this earth on my way to Heaven.

THE MALICE OF BIGOTRY

High in the sky, like an eagle,
Ride the thermals, transcend the mountain,
Soar the heavens on fluffy clouds, carefree, and merry,
Gloom and heartache unknown entities,
Lush and productive valley beneath seems eternal,
Happiness unspeakable, life a fragrant breeze,
Such is the heart's joy in a fertile season– full of life.
How man visions,
When life is surging

Anon, thermal dissipates, wind dies,
Plunging, plummeting, descend from the peaks,
No longer soaring, but falling like a wingless bird,
Mountain becomes a merciless volcano,
Molten lava wields death and destruction,
Red hot ash covers the terrain;
Fertile valley mutates from Spring to Winter– life to death.
How man's bigotry,
Yields malicious brutality.

Rudolf Hoess

RUDOLF FRANZ HOESS WAS born on November 25, 1900 in Baden-Baden, a town in southwest Germany, and died on April 16, 1947 in Auschwitz (Oswiecim), Poland. He was the eldest of three children, the only boy, and raised in a strict Catholic family where he grew up with the intention of entering the priesthood.

After the death of his father, he joined the German army in 1916, was wounded three times, and awarded the Iron Cross twice. Joining the East Prussian Free Corps in 1920, he took part in suppressing the conflicts in Latvia and in subduing workers who were staging an uprising in Ruhr. Through the Free Corps, he was introduced to Adolf Hitler in 1922.

When joining the Nazi Party, he renounced his affiliation with the Catholic Church. He joined the SS in 1933 and was attached to the SS at Dachau Concentration Camp in 1934 in Germany. In early 1940, he was appointed as the Commandant of Auschwitz in Poland.

In May of 1941, Hoess was told by Heinrich Himmler, the SS commander, that Hitler had given orders for the *final solution* or complete extermination of Jewry in Europe. Because it was considered a "secret Reich matter," Hoess was told not to speak about it with any person. It was Himmler's decision that this *final solution* would take place at Auschwitz, and Hoess immediately converted it into an extermination camp by installing gas chambers and crematoria (cremation facility).

It was a subordinate, Karl Fritzsch, that introduced Hoess to a pesticide called Zyklon B, a toxic gas from hydrogen cyanide into the killing process. It had been used in Germany before to disinfect ships, barracks, clothing, warehouses, factories, granaries, etc.

Zyklon B was produced in crystal form that produced amethyst-blue pellets. Because the pellets turned into a highly poisonous gas when exposed to air, they were stored and transported in sealed metal canisters.

Jewish and other undesirables who arrived by train to the camp were selected for the gas chambers. The victims were led to believe they had to be disinfected and bathed before entering the camp. After they had undressed for their shower, they were led to a camouflaged gas chamber containing fake shower heads. The large doors were sealed, and the prisoners were trapped inside. An orderly who wore a mask, opened a vent on the roof of the gas chamber, poured the Zyklon B pellets down the shaft, and then closed the vent to seal the gas chamber.

Immediately, the Zyklon B pellets turned into a deadly gas. Inside the chamber, the prisoners panicking and gasping for air, would shove, ram, and climb over each other to reach the door. With no way out, all inside were dead in three to fifteen minutes depending upon climatic conditions. Hoess stated at his trial that they knew the prisoners were dead when the screaming ceased. They waited about a half hour before opening the doors.

This process was considered to be a quick exterminator capable of exterminating 2,000 individuals at a time. Because the people believed they were going to take a shower, there was no need of guards to drive them into the gas chambers. After the long ride in cattle cars, they welcomed a shower.

Hoess aware of millions of innocent human beings murdered in the gas chambers, burned in the crematoriums, their teeth fillings melted into gold bars, wrote poetry about the *beauty* of Auschwitz.

At his trial, Hoess claimed that four large gas chambers and crematoria were constructed in Birkenau to make the killing more efficient, and to handle the increasing rate of killings. He alleged that it would have been possible to exterminate greater numbers, as the murdering itself took the least time. It was possible to dispose of 2,000 in half an hour. However, the burning of the bodies is what took the time. Hoess estimated that about 2,500,000 people were executed and exterminated at Auschwitz by gassing and burning, and about one-half-million died of starvation and disease.

He further claimed that they were required to carry out these exterminations in secrecy, however the foul and nauseating stench from the continuous burning of bodies permeated the entire area and all of the people living in the surrounding communities knew that exterminations were going on at Auschwitz.

On April 10, 1947, Hoess returned to the Catholic Church, received the sacrament of penance, and on the next day was administered the Holy Communion. Four days before he was executed, Hoess claimed his conscience compelled him to declare his grave sin against humanity, that he was responsible for carrying out the plans of the *Third Reich* for human destruction, and that he caused unspeakable suffering for the Polish people. He then asked the Lord God to forgive him, and intreated the forgiveness of the Polish people. However, it must be noted he didn't ask forgiveness for his debased cruelty to the Jews, Russians, Gypsies (Roma), etc. that were exterminated.

After the Nuremberg trial, Hoess was handed over to Polish authorities. There he was tried for murder by the Supreme National Tribunal and found guilty. On April 16, 1947, he was hanged on a gallows at Auschwitz facing the sign he had placed over the gate saying, *Arbeit Macht Frei.*

Eighth Letter

Dear Mama,

Sometimes I seem to be in a state of confusion as to what I believe. At times, I find myself crying out to God for strength to continue until I've finished my course. He always reminds me that his grace is sufficient for me to overcome.

Yet, there are moments that I feel as though my faith is hanging on by a thread. During those times, a fear that I won't overcome tries to consume me. But the Holy Spirit quickens my spirit that God has not given me a spirit of fear, but of power, and of love, and of a sound mind. It's a battle to surmount such turmoil of soul. But I truly know that I can do all things through Christ which strengtheneth me.

It's strange how easy it used to be to live the scriptures. I thought there were times that I was tested or facing a storm. But, Mama, it's quite clear that I had no comprehension of what persecution, tribulation, or a real storm of faith really was. At this time and in this place, I can truthfully attest that I know what it's like to be persecuted and faced with an incredible storm of hate and bigotry.

At least when Radoslaw was here, family times were remembered. We'd share our memories with each other to keep our spirits up with happy times. Radoslaw had an amazing ability to bring forth the comical things that happened at our family gatherings. Sometimes, we'd laugh ourselves and those listening to sleep.

I keep trying to reinforce my faith with Scripture. I seem to be on a see-saw. I'm up, then I'm down. Lack of food causes me to be unable to function and think properly at times. You always taught us the importance of a well-balanced diet to acquire the proper nutrients necessary for health and proper brain function. I'm fed a bitter beverage for breakfast, at noon, I receive a thin soup made from rotten vegetables or meat, and a crust of bread and a little portion of margarine before going to bed.

Although it's a diet of malnutrition, I know that my giving thanks for what he's supplied is causing my body to be blessed. He's impressed me that I'm not finished bringing others to faith in him. It does seem like they die that day or the next day or so. But I rejoice they are with him. I must admit there are many more that reject him. However, the Lord gave me peace that I've done my part, and he is pleased with me.

Lately, I sense a deterioration within my body. However, at the same time, I'm reminded of his promise that his strength is made perfect in weakness. Without the Holy Spirit reminding me of the promises, I would be like many in here who believe God has forsaken them.

Yesterday, a young man that I had just brought to the Lord was shot in front of me. He fell and couldn't get up from starvation and exhaustion. Just before he died, he looked at me, smiled, and mouthed, "I see Jesus!" It was like I had been given extra grace, for I truly felt rejuvenated.

Whatever God has planned for me, I know his love will get me through as it did the early church. His word promises that nothing can separate me from the love of God in Christ Jesus.

I miss you all so much.

Your loving son,

Stefan

P. S. I was watching a tree during a storm and it vacillated back and forth. However, its roots were deep, and it was standing strong after the storm. The Lord showed me that's how I'll get through this ordeal victoriously. My roots have to remain deep in his love.

A DREAM IN THE NIGHT

I dreamed a dream I did not know;
That found me in a troubled sea.
My memory was but a shadow;
What could have been so blood thirsty?

I'd heard chronicles of such things,
That imprisoned fellows who slept.
Unseen beasts without angel's wings,
From out of the oppression crept.

Powerless to get my bearing,
Something was fastening inside.
It was to my reason clutching;
My soul needed a place to hide.

I thought I understood my dreams,
Till this beast overshadowed me.
In the aloofness were my screams,
As if, via them, I would flee.

I discovered an unknown road;
My mind was shuffled in a storm.
At times, I saw a path of old,
Then it took on another form.

I heard in the earlier days,
Things were ascertained much clearer.
Perceived was a beast and its ways;
Why didn't such knowledge come nearer?

I knew that man oft walked the edge;
Wrong step taken, he plundered deep.
Had I traveled beyond the ledge,
Or was I really fast asleep?

I needed to remain afloat;
Where had the creature entered from?
Why did it take hold of my throat;
Was I bound for an asylum?

I seemed confused inside the dream,
Engulfed in billows that strangled.
With pressure, I was pulled downstream,
All spirit about diminished.

I struggled for something to hold,
But the current took me under.
My conception was uncontrolled,
All reason was put asunder.

I wailed as loud as I could;
It sounded forth but a whisper.
My faith discerned earth where I stood;
No longer was I to dicker.

I grabbed hold of reality,
And to it, I did adhere tight.
It jerked itself to be set free,
But I determined to see light.

I beheld the bits of reason,
That were jettisoned to and fro,
Migrating in my direction,
As they formed a new embryo.

SECTION IV

I wasn't certain what to do,
But comprehended faith and reason,
Joined with veracity, I knew,
Against these had been my treason.

Once rationality controlled;
I beheld a flash of great light.
No longer were my thoughts absurd;
Around faith, I dug a deep mote.

The creature let go of my throat;
My whisper became a loud scream.
Ended was the beast of the night;
Faith and truth defeated the dream.

SECTION V

"Faith is to believe what you do not see; the reward
of faith is to see what you believe."

—Saint Augustine

Heinrich Himmler

HEINRICH HIMMLER WAS BORN on October 7, 1900 in Munich, Germany into a middle-class Catholic family and died on May 23, 1945. His father was a demanding Roman Catholic secondary schoolmaster who had tutored the Bavarian Crown Prince.

After World War I, Himmler studied agriculture from Munich Technical High School. He joined the rightist paramilitary organizations, and joined the Nazi Party in 1925, where he rose steadily in the party's hierarchy. In 1930, he was elected a deputy of the German parliament (Reichstag). He was made Commander of all political police units outside of Prussia in March of 1933.

Himmler, in April of 1934, was appointed assistant chief of the Gestapo (Secret State Police) in Prussia. However, the real turning point of his career was his masterminding of the purge on June 30, 1934 that smashed the power of the SA and made way for the emergence of the SS as an independent organization and translated the racism of the regime into a forceful source of action.

He set up the first concentration camp in Dachau in 1933, and the next few years, with Hitler's encouragement were spent extending the range of persons who were suitable for confinement in the camps. Himmler had a belligerent mania with mesmerism (hypnotism), the occult, herbal remedies, and homeopathy that were in accord with his prejudiced obsessive racialism and commitment to the *Aryan* illusion.

The expansion of Himmler's empire and the means at his command were brought about by World War II. He was determined to safeguard the reality of a race society of "Aryan" supremacy by the methodical execution of Jews and Slavs in Poland and Russia. He was assigned to head the German anti-partisan campaign in the occupied areas that targeted racial and political enemies of the Third Reich and was distinguished by extensive acts of mass murder and brutality. It was Himmler who organized the extermination camps in German-occupied Poland where millions of Jews were systematically exterminated. Also, the camps provided workers for forced labor and people for forced medical experiments.

Himmler's dream was to cultivate a race of blue-eyed, tall, blond supermen through breeding a racially organized order. As the *Reichsfuhrer* (Reich Leader) of the SS, He introduced the principle of racial selection and special marriage laws which would ensure the systematic coupling of people that would generate the supremacy of the *Aryan* race or German people. His establishing the State-registered human stud farm, where young girls selected for their perfect Nordic traits could procreate with SS men, displayed Himmler's mania to create a race of *supermen* by means of reproduction.

He indoctrinated the SS with an apocalyptic morality absent of guilt and responsibility, thereby, justifying mass murder as a form of martyrdom and harshness towards oneself. Himmler believed that whether other races lived in comfort or perish of hunger was of no interest to him. He was only concerned with their need as slaves for Germany's culture. He could care less if Russian woman collapse from exhaustion while digging a ditch as long the ditch was completed.

Himmler taught that Germans were the only people in the world with a decent attitude towards animals and would adopt such an attitude towards the human animals. However, it would be a crime against their own blood to worry about them and to bring them value. He believed the extermination of the Jewish people was of the utmost importance. Because of his beliefs, Hitler entrusted Himmler with the planning and implementation of the "Final Solution."

When Himmler became aware that the war was being lost, he met with the representative of the World Jewish Congress to discuss openings for negotiations of peace without Hitler's knowledge. Upon hearing of this, in April of 1945, Hitler dismissed him from all his posts and ordered his arrest.

At the end of the war, Himmler attempted to go into hiding. However, on May 20, 1945, dressed in a Secret Field Police uniform with papers claiming to be Heinrich Hitzinger, he was captured by Russian soldiers and turned over to the British where he eventually confessed who he was. While undergoing a body search on May 23, 1945, Himmler committed suicide by biting down on a capsule of cyanide poisoning hidden in his mouth.

Final Letter

Dear Mama,

This will be my last letter from Auschwitz. Earlier, the strangest thing happened. A new doctor, Josef Mengele who is called the "Angel of death" walked by me. I'd never seen him before and have no idea why he was there. I knew it was him because of his crisp uniform, his riding crop, and meticulously polished black boots.

Anyway, he looked at me with this sinister smile. As he walked away, the Lord told me that I'm to be set free. My body has weakened, and I know I'll not make it through another day in the manufacturing of synthetic rubber.

Because you are so in tune with the Holy Spirit, I'm sure you've already heard. Know that I feel complete peace in the Lord. In truth, I have never experienced such serenity. It's like a taste of Heaven.

I wanted to thank you for your prayers, for encouraging me in the faith, and for teaching me that hope triumphs in the end. I leave here with peace of mind, despite the evil inflicted, the turmoil of soul, and the battle that has raged within.

The Lord has blessed me with the highest triumph. I have forgiven each and every one of them. Praise God, I have no chains of unforgiveness, hate, malice, etc. I prayed for them all, and I realize that it's my captives who are chained. Their self-love, hate, and unbridled bigotry have harvested an incredible evil. May they recognize their cruelty to their fellow humanity, repent, turn to Christ for forgiveness, and be unchained.

Mama, my heart's no longer heavy. I can barely contain my excitement. I find myself overjoyed with love and thankfulness to the Lord for his grace that brought me through like the early church. I've faced the lion and have overcome.

Now, the words of Sydney Carten ring loudly that "it is a far, far better rest that I go to, than I have ever known."

Your eternal son,
Stefan

FORGIVENESS

Forgive us our faults, as we forgive others.
When smitten, turn the other cheek.
Taught for faith to please God, must forgive.
Faith is the victory that overcomes the world.
Forgiveness is greater than unforgiveness.
Hate and unforgiveness are detrimental,
Ravaging leeches, a cancerous, parasitical blight.
In essence,
They are self-destructive.

Oftentimes, anger seethes.
Indignation rises like a vaporous cloud of hate,
Hot and scalding, aimed with animosity, at merciless beast,
Embodiment of villainy, assailant of defenseless,
Innocent victims, faultless, guiltless of wrong.
Struggling against becoming a clone of my captors,
I remember I am forgiven only as I forgive.
In essence,
Forgiveness is the highest triumph!

SECTION VI

"Bad men need nothing more to compass their ends, than
that good men should look on and do nothing."

—John Stuart Mill (1867)

Conclusion

IF WE TAKE A sincere look around at what is happening in America and the rest of the world, we are in danger of our rights and our right to choose being taken away from us. Freedom is a word that has been synonymous with America, but the socialist agenda of the liberal left intends to make "freedom" a byword for the majority of the population. What do I mean by that? We have those pushing for socialism where the right to privately own property is forbidden. In other words, we are no longer free to own our own business or our own house, etc. The government owns and controls everything, and it's no longer "We the people" who have any voice. It's the government who not only possesses and regulates everything, but who has the *only* voice. We either fall in line with them or we are considered enemies of the state.

I'm not trying to be a voice of woe, but one of enlightenment. The mentality of many today is receiving "free stuff" whether it's medical, food stamps, education, etc. However, NOTHING is ever free. It always costs someone. Our salvation is free to us, but what a cost it was to Christ.

The "free stuff" mentality creates slothfulness, idleness, laziness in people who no longer have to work for what they receive. What kind of reward is there in having things handed to us without any self-effort on our part? Don't get me wrong. I believe that some of us can fall upon difficult times and need a helping hand to get back on our feet. However, it's not a way of life for us. We believe in working for what we attain. There's an inner satisfaction when we earn something through our effort.

Yet, "free stuff" without effort or work is the kind of mentality that the liberals are promoting in our country. The liberals propagating socialism seem to believe that it's not important who is hurt (financially) by the outrageous socialist agenda. Some are advocating for the government to control even our utility companies. They believe in overtaxing like California is currently doing.

Look at the homeless population in that state because of the governmental taxing and regulations. Yet, one of them is a millionaire who uses air travel, advocates the "new green deal" that would raise energy prices, slow economic growth, reduce wages, and promote climate control. Furthermore, this socialist believes that climate change is real, catastrophic, and largely caused by human activities.

Let me tell you, the Bible makes clear that God upholds (sustains, supports, maintains, nurtures) all things by the word of his power (Hebrews 1:3). Climate change activists believe that man controls this Universe, they leave God out of the equation. It's God who spoke all things into existence (Genesis 1), and man will NOT be the one who destroys this earth.

> But the day of the Lord will come as a thief in the night, in the which the heavens shall pass away with a great noise, and the elements shall melt with fervent heat, the earth also and the works that are therein shall be burned up (II Peter 5:10).

It's God who will initiate a *global warming*, not man. It's time for Christians to read and study their Bibles and not be instigated by lies and propaganda. A proper knowledge of Scripture will give the wisdom needed to recognize the fake news being promoted by the liberals who endorse a socialist agenda.

It seems liberals running for president, have one goal, and that's to be president. Whatever has to be done to destroy this nation is what they'll do to attain their ambition. We need to comprehend that any president must be for the betterment of our country, promoting the American dream, against the murder of babies, against making people government dependent (this sets them up to take the anti-Christ's mark), keeping illegals (law-breakers) from having access to our country, strong border protection, and wants God to bless America.

If we think about it, the liberals are doing exactly what Hitler did. Germany was destroyed by this self-lover who used propaganda at the cost of the people and the country. He promoted unbridled bigotry until an incredible evil was harvested. I'm not saying that the socialist candidates are promoting hate and prejudice on that scale, but one of them has proven to be anti-Semitic. He's certainly endorsing socialist, communist, and authoritarian nations like Cuba, Soviet Union, Venezuela, etc.

Furthermore, we have Muslims in our government pushing sharia law that teaches to kill anyone who rejects Islam, converts to Christianity, or becomes an atheist. To further explain, it's important to note that in countries that are run by sharia law, the constitution becomes inferior to the Islamist laws of the land. When radical Islam gains power, every article in the constitution becomes contingent on compliance with sharia. The rights that are promised in the constitution become null and void. In other words, only those following Islam are allowed the right to live. This truth was seen in Nazi Germany. Only those who were part of Nazism had the right to live.

We have others in government positions who are trying to remove our constitutional rights. These rights include the freedom of speech, freedom of religion, the right to keep and bear arms, the freedom of assembly, and the freedom to petition. It also prohibits unreasonable search and seizure, cruel and unusual punishment, and compelled self-incrimination. Yet, the liberals have continuously broken, ignored, or wrongly interpreted the Constitutional laws of our country.

The intention of this book is to convey that self-love will reap a holocaust of evil resulting in man's cruelty to humanity. With the rise of anti-Semitism, racism, and bigotry in general, I believe, we, as human beings, must take a closer look at what is happening around us. Any prolonged prejudice against a group of people will lead to those obsessed with hate to seek the annihilation of those they believe to be inferior. All we have to do is look at what happened after Donald J. Trump was lawfully elected. There were riots claiming he wasn't their president. We have reverted into a country where the liberals will not accept what they don't want. The government has become a circus of feeding bigotry and hate against the president and those who voted for him, instead of serving the people they are supposed to represent.

What I'm endeavoring to reveal is that we must learn from history. When good men sit by and allow evil to run rampant, it will thrive. Hitler and the Nazis were permitted to go unchecked until it was a consuming evil. We must wake up to what is being propagated in our government and vote it out before it consumes this *One Nation Under God.*

It's time to stand against the evil infiltrating America and be the loudest voices that overcome those voices out to destroy. Christians must comprehend the spirit of bigotry is rising. If it is allowed to continue unbridled, it will consume every area of our Nation and our freedom as we know it.

When we look back at the Holocaust, we can't help but see an illustrative manifestation of absolute evil. It revealed the power of malevolent social and governmental forms and disclosed what occurs when the depth of human nature is allowed to be controlled by its affinity towards self-love, selfishness, wickedness, bigotry, hatred, anti-God, etc.

Many survivors report hearing a specific final plea from those who were killed by the Nazis: "Remember! Do not let the world forget." To this responsibility, survivors have added an appeal of their own: "Never again! Never for the Jewish people. Never for *any* people."

It is the hope of survivors that remembrance of the Holocaust can avoid its reappearance. In part, because of their efforts, interest in the horrors of the Nazi endeavor to exterminate the Jewish population in Europe has increased rather than diminished with the passage of time. Many countries observe Holocaust remembrance days each year. More than half a century after the Holocaust, institutions, memorials, and museums continue to be built and films and educational programs created to document and teach the history of the Holocaust for future generations.

To Christians in America, it's time for us to pay close attention to what is happening in our government. Each time one of our Constitutional rights is infringed, it brings us closer to socialism, communism, and perhaps sharia law ruling our country. It was the looking the other way, by many, that enabled Hitler and the Nazis to become a ruthless power.

The rise in those promoting socialism, if not nipped in the bud, could turn our beloved country into a socialist nation. If that is allowed to happen, it will slow economic growth, reduce entrepreneurial opportunity and competition, and create a lack of purpose by individuals due to a decreased recompense.

Venezuela was once a prosperous country until it fell into the hands of socialism. Now, it's full of political corruption, chronic shortages of food and medicine, termination of companies, unemployment, deterioration of production, dictatorship, violation of human rights, gross economic mishandling, etc.

This is the result of socialism that is not being addressed by the liberal left in America advocating it. It becomes a one-party ruling government that caters to a certain group of people, and becomes a dictatorship as in Nazi Germany. While the elite of the government live in luxury, the rest of population lives in poverty, lack, and ruin.

Christians must stand in the way of the liberal left's debauched propaganda. We must be a wall against abortion (murder of unborn and born babies); we must be a wall against the increase of homosexuality (men with men and women with women); we must be a wall against transgender (belief that a male lives inside a female or a female lives inside a male); we must be a wall against child sex, pornography, and the sins that will not inherit the kingdom of God. For more about these declarations, read my books: *Signs of the Time* and *Spiritual Shipwreck on the Horizon*.

We are told in Scripture those who pray for the peace of Jerusalem and love her shall prosper (Psalms 122:6). God blesses those who bless Israel and curses all that curse her, for in Israel (Abraham) came Jesus who is the greatest of all God's blessings.

At this time, I want to add some statements past and present about socialism. In 1975, Ronald Reagan said this: "Socialist ignore the side of man that is of the spirit. They can provide shelter, fill your belly with bacon and beans, treat you when you're ill—all the things that are guaranteed to a prisoner or a slave. But they don't understand we also dream, yes, even of owning a yacht." Christians must not allow our capitalist form of government that allows us to follow the American dream be destroyed by socialism, communism, or sharia law.

Recently, Mark Levin of "Life, Liberty, and Levin" said this in a tweet: "My fellow conservatives, there's nothing to celebrate about Sanders' victory and possible, if not likely nomination." Although he did not elaborate on that tweet, on the February 18, 2020 edition of Premiere Radio Networks: *The Mark Levin Show* he said: "The man leading the Democrat Party right now is embracing an Islamo-Nazi mentality when it comes to the Jewish state. And the kind of people Bernie Sanders is pulling around him could come out of the Third Reich." And last month, Levin said on radio that Sanders is a Marxist who supports the most vile Marxist regimes. . .He praised Cuba. He praised the Soviet Union. He praised Venezuela. And this is not being reported.

President Trump's campaign adviser Mercedes Schlapp made the case against socialism at the Conservative Political Action Conference (CPAC) in February of 2020 where she blasted socialism and warned that Republicans must "stop it in its tracks." She went on to say, "We live in the greatest country in the world. Our democracy is fragile, our freedoms are fragile, and what we have seen in history, is that those freedoms can be swiftly taken away from the individual. We've seen it country after country. . .Our democracy and freedom is under threat. And we have an obligation to save America from the horrible ideology of socialism. As we know, socialism leads to communism."

To reveal what I mean about the propagation of socialism, Bernie Sanders had this to say in a recent interview on CBS News. He claimed that not everything under Castro (the Cuban dictator) is bad. In other words, this socialist is claiming there's good in evil.

Mercedes Schlapp fired back at Sanders' statement by telling the story of her father's imprisonment by the Havana regime. She stated, "The goal of socialism ends up being communism, which is government takeover of the individual. It not only includes health-care, it includes freedom of speech."

Her father being imprisoned in Cuba for his "political beliefs" confirmed the "dangers of socialist-communist" government. Her father lost everything he worked for. His being put in jail because of his political beliefs, shows the dangers of socialist governments, of communist governments where they not only ration food, but take away your guns.

Recently, President Donald J. Trump at a speech to the UN General Counsel on September 19, 2017, said, "Wherever true socialism has been adopted, it has delivered anguish, and devastation, and failure." Then on February 18, 2019 at the Florida International University, the President spoke to a Venezuelan-American audience, of which, many had experienced the absence of freedom and opportunity while living under a socialist regime. He said, "We know that socialism in not about justice, it's not about equality, it's not about lifting up the poor. Socialism is about one thing only: power for the ruling class. And the more power they get, the more they crave."

Let me help those who are reading this book to more fully understand the dangers of socialism. Before a country becomes socialist, it makes sure the citizens are defenseless against its tyranny. We must wake up to what the liberals are trying to do. They claim gun violence is why they want to take away our second amendment rights. However, it is to make sure that we are defenseless in defending our country against the oppression of socialism.

The Second Amendment of the United States Constitution says, "A well-regulated Militia, being necessary to the *security* OF A FREE STATE, the right of the people to keep and bear Arms, shall not be infringed."

Let me tell you this truth. If those bent on turning our country into socialism, communism succeed in taking away our second amendment constitutional right, they will be allowed to take away the *security* of any free state. That's why we must vote these liberals out of office before it turns into something like Cuba, Venezuela, Nazi Germany, etc. Each of those countries made sure the people had NO means of resisting the government's agenda to inject socialism and communism in their country.

It's not equality that socialism is for, but making sure the ruling class (those in government or working with them) rules and all others are subservient and docile through fear and whatever it takes to keep us quiet. Removing our right to bear arms is the first step in a government takeover. Then they remove all our constitutional rights, and our voice is silenced.

It's imperative that we learn from history. If we look closely at what the liberals are promoting, we must conclude it's a resurgence of what happened in Germany where only those considered worthy were the *Aryan* race. It was only those who agreed with the Nazi mentality that were allowed to survive. All political dissidents, handicapped, non *Aryan* were considered as subhuman or human animals and expendable. Seriously, is not that the liberal mentality? Babies are considered as expendable, conservatives are considered the enemy, Trump voters are attacked verbally and physically.

Let's not be deceived that socialism is superior to capitalism. Our capitalist system allows for an economic and political system in which a country's trade and industry are controlled by private owners for profit, rather than by the state. To explain, capitalism is an economic system where the government plays a *secondary* role. The people and companies have the *primary* role of making most of the decisions, and own most of the property.

Abraham Lincoln, when speaking at Gettysburg, in honor of the soldiers that sacrificed their lives in the war, stated, "That government of the people, by the people, for the people, shall not perish from the earth." That's what our constitutional republic is all about. It's the people who vote (choose) who is in government. These officials work for us, they are not to dictate our lives. Yet, we see "We the People" having less and less voice in matters. Local governments are deciding how and what we are allowed to do. Those in federal government are striving to silence any voice that is contrary to their liberal, socialist, etc. beliefs.

Christian, patriot, God-fearing Americans, if we don't rise against this evil trying to destroy this great nation founded on freedom of the individual and not freedom of the government to control us, we will be like Venezuela or other third world countries. We will be stripped of all our Constitutional rights, our voice will be silenced, and we will be void of the American dream.

Socialism is a breeding ground for corruption, bureaucracy, and favoritism. The State holds the majority of the power which is often abused for personal gains. It essentially restricts the freedom of its citizens who are imprisoned under its power.

I believe some have received a taste of restricted freedoms during the Covid-19 pandemic. Many have complained and rebelled against the restrictions. Yet, all this only gives a glimpse of the freedoms lost under Socialism. People were frustrated by several weeks of restrictions for health reasons. Whereas, Socialism is a life of restrictions and governmental rule for the sake of oppressing its people.

Let me explain further the difference between capitalism and socialism. Under our capitalist system, production is largely or entirely privately owned by individuals or companies and operate for profit. Characteristics central to capitalism include private property, capital accrual, wage labor, voluntary exchange, a price system, and competitive markets. It has many benefits compared to other economic forms. It actively rewards positive traits like hard work and ingenuity. Similarly, capitalism punishes negative traits such as laziness and theft. Whereas, socialism promoting welfare dependence encourages the people to become lazy and unproductive and never comprehend the pride of self-dependence. Furthermore, socialism requires government interference and control. Whereas, capitalism doesn't require any interference from the government and can develop naturally.

When good men and women sit by and allow evil to run rampant, it will thrive. Evil begins as a little leaven until it has consumed the whole. This is seen in that all the Democrat candidates that were running in the 2020 presidential race favored infanticide or the killing the baby before and after birth. It's a *Holocaust* to exterminate the helpless, the unwanted, the problem, etc. Plus, it's a money making venture selling the body parts of babies. When comparing the atrocities of the Nazis, I see a more malevolent mentality in the liberals condoning and promoting abortion.

It's frightening to see how many favor socialism. These people have a wicked agenda to take away our Constitutional rights, eliminate the Electoral College, abolish religious rights, make us voiceless, and if necessary destroy those who disagree with their evil intentions.

Look at what's being done by the liberals, some are ordering the death of the President. Calling people to hostility against those who voted for him. How many times have we heard that someone has been assaulted by someone because they are a Trump supporter or wore a "Make America Great Again" hat. This is scary to say the least.

We must awaken out of our stupor and vote these people out of our government before we are no longer a *One Nation Under God*, but one of the socialist nations where the people are no longer given a voice, most live in abject poverty, and those in government live in luxury and wealth.

Please comprehend it's not loyalty to a political party. The mentality that my parents, my grandparents, etc. belonged to this political party, and that's why I do, reveals a lack of reason. We must wake-up and recognize our loyalty belongs to God, our children, our country, our Constitution, and our flag. It's our obligation, our responsibility, and our duty to make sure this country does NOT fall into the hands of socialism, communism, or sharia law.

IT'S TIME TO SEE WHAT IS COMING UPON OUR LAND AND BLOW THE TRUMPET TO WARN THE PEOPLE, lest we find ourselves living in a nightmare of freedoms and liberty lost!

Epilogue

"Progress, far from consisting in change,
depends on retentiveness... Those who cannot
remember the past are *condemned* to repeat it."

—George Santayana, *The Life of Reason* (1905–06).